AF254847

Sweater for Mr. Fetter

for Mr. Fetter

Christmas Story

by Sergiy Tovstenko and Tania King
pictures by Olena Kvitka

Whirligig Press

Sweater for Mr. Fetter
Copyright © 2019 by Sergiy Tovstenko and Tania King
Illustrations Copyright © 2019 by Olena Kvitka

Summary:"The story of a nine-year-old girl who is preparing for Christmas with her friends and persuades them to make a present for a lonely old man, but the children have to donate Christmas stockings and even favorite mittens."

ISBN: 978-0-578-60464-0
Library of Congress Control Number: 2019917871

Editor: Cassandra Ervin
Book designer: Irina Potapova

Printed in the U.S.A.

Sweater
for Mr. Fetter

Christmas Story

Hello!
My name is Miranda.
I am 9 years old, and
I love everything that is
colorful and bright.
I have a yellow jacket,
a green hat, and red
mittens.

My aunt Concordia
knitted my mittens.
They are the most
beautiful thing I have!
They are as bright and
colorful as Christmas.

Christmas is tomorrow. I like Christmas! I am sure I will receive bright and colorful presents! Right now, I am admiring my red mittens and our small and happy town. It is also bright, colorful, and festive!

Only the house across the street is gloomy.
I do not like it.

These are my friends Jessica, Dan, and Paul.
They also like colorful things.
Jessica has a lilac coat and a pink cap.
Dan has blue boots and an orange scarf.
Paul has a yellow hat and a purple jacket.

There is Mr. Fetter.
He is my neighbor and lives in that
gloomy house across the street.
He has a black coat.
He slouches and keeps his hands
in his pockets.
Maybe he does not have mittens.
He stands on his porch grumbling,
"IT IS TOO COLORFUL."

Jessica, Dan, Paul and I play in the snow outside.
We are sledding and shouting to everyone,
"Merry Christmas!"
They smile, and we smile.
It seems that even the winter sun is becoming brighter.

Mr. Fetter frowns at us grumbling,
"IT IS TOO SUNNY."

We are having a snowball fight.
Dan and I are one team,
and Jessica and Paul are the other team.
We run after one another, throwing
snowballs and laughing.
I like making the snowballs
and playing with my friends! It is fun!

Mr. Fetter walks past us with his
jacket covering his ears.
He is muttering,
"IT IS TOO NOISY."

My friends and I talk about Christmas.
We have already hung our Christmas stockings
by our families' fireplaces and are waiting for gifts.
I want to get a watercolor paint set.
Jessica would like a soft stuffed polar bear.
Paul asked Santa for a yellow construction truck.
Dan dreams about a blue mountain bike.

Mr. Fetter is walking back from a grocery store. He looks sad.
I wonder what he would like for Christmas?
Did he hang up his Christmas stocking by the fireplace?

People have decorated all the trees in the town with festive lights.
Only the fir tree growing opposite Mr. Fetter's house
is dark and dull.
I have an idea to decorate it!
Jessica and Dan bring a stepladder.
Paul and I bring colorful ornaments.

Mr. Fetter is on his porch.
He watches as we decorate the fir tree.
He is muttering,
"IT IS TOO FESTIVE."

Clouds fill the sky over the town and the wind blows.
Our decorated fir tree shakes and the festive branches rustle.
Thick snow falls from the sky.
We decide to build a snowman!
Our mittens keep our hands pleasantly warm as we form
the body of the snowman.

Mr. Fetter stays on his porch.
Perhaps he is interested in
looking at our snowman.
He buttons up his
black coat muttering,
"IT IS TOO SNOWY."

Our snowman is ready!
My aunt Concordia from the house next door waves at us.
She treats us to hot cocoa and gives us a bucket
to use as a hat for our snowman.
By the way, my aunt Concordia is a celebrity!
She is the fastest knitter in the world!
I again admire the red mittens that my aunt has knitted for me.

Mr. Fetter walks by my
aunt's window. He mutters
something again, but I
cannot hear him.
What is now
"TOO MUCH?"

We look at Mr. Fetter and try to guess what
he is grumbling about this time.
Paul jokes, "**THE STREET IS TOO CLEAN.**"
Dan jokes, "**THE SNOW IS TOO WHITE.**"
Jessica and I chuckle.
Aunt Concordia shakes her head and says
that Mr. Fetter is **TOO ALONE**.
All his relatives died, and no one has come
to visit him for a long time.
My friends and I feel ashamed.

So that's why Mr. Fetter is so bleak!
For a long time nobody has visited him.
For a long time he hasn't received
any Christmas presents.
Mr. Fetter is gloomy;
his house is gloomy;
his life is **GLOOMY TOO**.

We put the bucket on the snowman's
head, but now we are sad.
I cannot forget Aunt Concordia's words.
I look at my warm, red mittens and I have another idea!
I tell Jessica, Paul, and Dan.
They like my idea!
I wonder what Mr. Fetter will say.
Will he mutter that it is **TOO MUCH**?

We run home, and soon everyone brings their…
KNITTED CHRISTMAS STOCKINGS!
Then we got to the houses of our school mates.
Everyone worries a little: how will we get our
presents without Christmas stockings?
But all of us would like to please a lonely old man.

By evening we have lots of gorgeous Christmas stockings!
All of them are colorful!
We run to Aunt Concordia again and explain our idea to her.
She is surprised at first, but then she laughs and gets to work
at once.

Hurry up, dear Aunt Concordia!
Please, hurry up!
You are the fastest knitter in the world!

We are looking at the house
of Mr. Fetter.
It is dark and gloomy.
Only a faint light is visible in one window.
It is **TOO DIM AND WEAK…**

Knitting needles move in a flurry!
The item that Aunt Concordia is knitting is very colorful.
The **CHRISTMAS STOCKINGS** are so different, after all.
Finally, she finishes.

However, Aunt Concordia is looking around.
She needs the main decoration for this new thing.
She looks closely at my red mittens!
I... **HIDE** one of my beautiful, warm,
red mittens **DEEP IN MY POCKET.**

And the other one...
I give it to my aunt!
I want Mr. Fetter's life to be warmer.
Maybe he will not mutter that the thing is **TOO MUCH**.

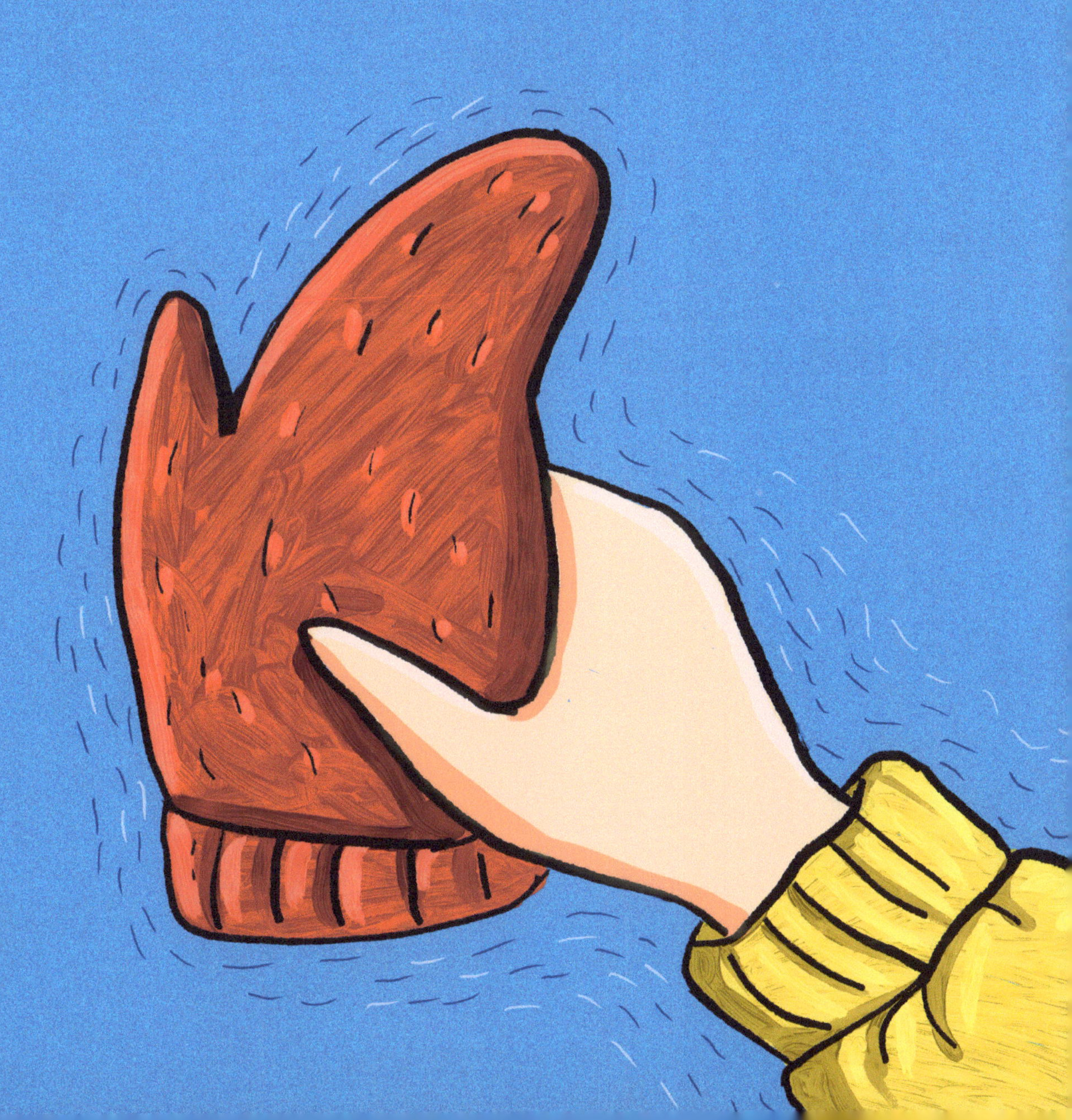

Night has fallen, but our street is shining with festive lights.
Together with Aunt Concordia, we cross the street to
Mr. Fetter's house and knock on the door.
All of us are a little nervous.
The door opens with a creak.
I hand Mr. Fetter a box tied with a shiny ribbon and bow.
"Merry Christmas, Mr. Fetter!" we all exclaim.

Mr. Fetter looks at us and blinks.
He is confused.
"IT IS TOO... UNEXPECTED," he says.
"IT IS TOO…NICE," he says.
"THANK YOU," he adds quietly.

Mr. Fetter opens the box. Inside is a sweater.
We ask him to try it on. The sweater looks great.
"Is not IT TOO COLORFUL?" Jessica asks.
"Is not IT TOO BRIGHT?" Dan asks.
"Is not IT TOO TIGHT?" Paul asks.
I do not have any questions. I look and see my red mItten.
It is over the heart of Mr. Fetter.
Aunt Concordia is the greatest
knitter ever!

Mr. Fetter says,
"This sweater is **TOO COMFORTABLE,
TOO WARM,** and **TOO CHRISTMASY.**
It is the best sweater
I have ever had."
Mr. Fetter smiles.

We walk back to our houses.
My right hand is freezing in the cold,
but I do not mind.
The snow clouds over the town move,
and the stars are now visible in the sky.
One of the constellations resembles
a mitten, and among all the stars
the brightest is the CHRISTMAS STAR.

This book is dedicated to the dreamers

The ones who stare out the window and dream about space.
The ones who doodle in their notebooks and dream about characters.
The ones who take apart alarm clocks and dream about robots.
The ones who see a problem and dream of solutions.
The ones who dream of a world better than today.
The ones who dream of equality for all of their friends.
The ones who dream of all the possibilities that lie ahead.
You will be amazing—just go out and do it.

Scott—thank you for dreaming with me and making this possible.
Grammie—thank you for making it possible to dream (and write).
Carrie—There are not enough thank you's in the world for all you have done as my "big sister".
My 3 families—You are big and you are loud and you are the reason I am who I am today.
Ronnie—thank you for being the dream I have been waiting for.
Natalie—thank you for your love of reading and giving me the idea for this dream.
Rehma, Emery, Anthony, Ryder, Walker, and future babies—I hope all of your dreams come true and that this book helps you find those dreams.

All *Dream It & Do It* research was done using only autobiographical materials. Please see the bibliography at www.dreamitandoit.com/bibliography. Role models were chosen that represent the rainbow of children in the world and those that had autobiographical materials available. All due diligence was used to provide only the most accurate information about the job itself and the role model used to highlight the job, however, if you believe there is a detail that deserves further attention, please reach the author at **dreamitanddoitbooks@gmail.com.**

Dream It & Do It – Kid Role Models is launching in the spring of 2021. If you know a child who would be a good role model, share their story on Instagram or Facebook with #dreamit&doit. For updates on this book launch, follow us or join our mail list at **www.dreamitandoit.com.**

FIRST EDITION